The Spider
or the Fly?

by Sam Bobrick

A SAMUEL FRENCH ACTING EDITION

SAMUEL FRENCH

FOUNDED 1830

NEW YORK HOLLYWOOD LONDON TORONTO

SAMUELFRENCH.COM

MUSIC USE NOTE

Licensees are solely responsible for obtaining formal written permission from copyright owners to use copyrighted music in the performance of this play and are strongly cautioned to do so. If no such permission is obtained by the licensee, then the licensee must use only original music that the licensee owns and controls. Licensees are solely responsible and liable for all music clearances and shall indemnify the copyright owners of the play and their licensing agent, Samuel French, Inc., against any costs, expenses, losses and liabilities arising from the use of music by licensees.

IMPORTANT BILLING AND CREDIT
REQUIREMENTS

All producers of *THE SPIDER OR THE FLY?* *must* give credit to the Author of the Play in all programs distributed in connection with performances of the Play, and in all instances in which the title of the Play appears for the purposes of advertising, publicizing or otherwise exploiting the Play and/ or a production. The name of the Author *must* appear on a separate line on which no other name appears, immediately following the title and *must* appear in size of type not less than fifty percent of the size of the title type.

THE SPIDER OR THE FLY? was first presented unde the name ***THE STANWAY CASE*** by the Tree Trunk Theatrical Company at the Horseshoe Theater in Van Nuys, California in February 2003. The performance was directed by Aaron J. Bronsal. The cast was as follows:

MAURA . . . . Lori Murphy
SCOTT. . . . . Tripp Pickell
TOM . . . . Keith Patterson
JAN . . . . Shannan Leigh

CHARACTERS

(in order of appearance)

MAURA

SCOTT

JAN

TOM

The characters are all in their early to mid-thirties. The actors playing Jan and Tom can play the two unidentified characters that appear in the Prologue. Care should be taken so that their faces cannot be seen.

SETTING

Except for the prologue, which takes place in a dimly lit space on stage, the entire play takes place in Maura Finley's one-room New York City apartment.

TIME

ACT I

Scene 1

Early evening.

Scene 2

The next night. Early evening.

Scene 3

Several days later. Early evening.

ACT II

Scene 1

A Saturday afternoon. Two weeks later.

AUTHOR'S NOTES

Special attention should be paid to the lighting cues.

"Come into my parlor", said the spider to the fly...
Mary Howitt (1799-1888)

PROLOGUE

*(A small portion of the stage is dimly lit so that we can
see the silhouette of the back of a woman in a negligee
slowly brushing her long hair. It is a sensuous moment.
Eerie music begins to sneak in. Suddenly behind the
woman, the silhouette of a man appears and surrepti-
tiously approaches the unsuspecting woman. He holds
something in his hand. A brick. The music grows louder.
Once he is directly behind her, he lifts the brick over her
head. Sensing a presence, the woman turns, looks up
and screams as she sees the man bring the brick down on
her head. As she falls to the floor he continues hitting her
again and again. The music comes to a loud climax.)*

(blackout)

ACT ONE

Scene 1

(Time: The Present. A warm spring evening.)

(The scene: The entire play takes place in Maura Finley's charming one-room first floor apartment in an old reconverted New York brownstone. Upstage center are French doors that face the street and open onto a narrow balcony. Only the two center doors need to open. The doors are the only window area in the apartment but enough to make the room seem bright and inviting. On each side of the doors are bookcases filled with books. A wine rack holding several bottles of wine sits on a shelf on the stage left bookcase. The apartment's front door is located upstage right. Further down is another door which leads to a walk in closet. Stage left is a door leading to the bathroom. Further downstage is a galley kitchen, which is hidden behind folding doors. The room is furnished quite warmly, yet there are no family photos displayed nor an abundance of knickknacks. In the center of the room and facing the audience is a sofa bed with a coffee table in front. There are two comfortable sitting chairs around the coffee table. Upstage left is a desk with a swivel desk chair. On top of the desk there is a computer, printer, desk lamp, telephone, answering machine and a cup filled with pens and pencils.)

*(At Rise: The room is dim, lit only by what early evening light comes through the French doors. The front door opens and **MAURA FINLEY**, a woman in her early thirties enters, followed by **SCOTT HAGEN**, about the same age. **MAURA** switches on the light. Although attractive, **MAURA** seems to go out of her way to hide it. Everything*

about her is quite conservative, almost prudish, her hair; her clothes. **SCOTT**, *on the other hand seems to go out of his way to capture a somewhat boyish charm.)*

SCOTT. *(Looking around room, impressed.)* Hey. This is nice. Very nice.

MAURA. I'm glad you like it. Like I said it's only one room but it has everything I need.

SCOTT. Yeah, I do like it. I like it a lot.

MAURA. Yes. Everyone seems to. Everyone who's seen it. Actually not many people have. I'm not much on entertaining even though the room is quite conducive to it.

SCOTT. I feel very privileged.

MAURA. The truth is, I'm really a very private person.

SCOTT. I sort of sensed that talking to you at dinner. It seemed I had to pry almost every word out of you and I didn't get that many. I haven't figured out whether it's a severe case of shyness or insecurity.

MAURA. Actually, it's caution. I usually loosen up a bit once I get to know people a little better.

SCOTT. And trust them.

MAURA. Maybe.

SCOTT. *(Quickly scans the room again.)* Well, it's a great apartment. Very Parisian.

MAURA. Have you been to Paris?

SCOTT. No, but I've seen a lot of foreign movies which kind of gets you there. How about you?

MAURA. No, I'm ashamed to admit, as yet I haven't. But I am planning to go one day. I have a feeling I'll find Paris very agreeable.

SCOTT. Can I make a suggestion?

MAURA. Of course.

SCOTT. I think you shouldn't use words like agreeable. That's a sixty-year-old librarian's word. I think someone your age should use words like "cool" or "hot."

MAURA. Actually, I do. When I'm talking about the weather.

(She goes to the two doors which hide the galley kitchen, opens them, and begins preparing coffee.)

Is decaf okay?

SCOTT. If you make it strong enough.

MAURA. I was really torn about asking you up here, considering the fact that we just met today. But our dinner was over so soon and then when you picked up the check, I felt you at least had an invitation for coffee coming. Besides, I believe it's common knowledge that if a woman did have amorous intentions it would have been an invitation for a glass of wine instead of a cup of coffee.

SCOTT. I wasn't aware of that.

MAURA. Well, now you are. Anyway, I do wish you would have let me pay my half. When you suggested dinner together you said we would be going as colleagues rather than two people with romantic hopes.

SCOTT. I guess I'm from that old school that still believes a man should always get stuck with the check. And with that fifteen dollars a day we're getting for jury duty, I was really feeling flush. Besides, if it will make you feel better, I did have romantic hopes.

MAURA. Really? At what point?

SCOTT. Immediately after you said "yes" to my invitation. *(Sits on sofa.)* I take it this is a sofa bed.

MAURA. Yes. But I very seldom open it. I usually just throw my sheets and blankets right over the top and sleep on it that way.

SCOTT. It doesn't say much for your sex life.

MAURA. Actually it does.

SCOTT. Yeah, great apartment. Everything so neat, so in its place, so carefully perfect which is just the way you first impressed me.

MAURA. Oh. *(She sits on the sofa.)*

SCOTT. By any chance was there anything about me that first impressed you?

MAURA. No. Not really.

SCOTT. Oh.

MAURA. Actually at first I was really put off by you. You seemed much too outgoing to be sincere.

SCOTT. A very disturbing observation. What finally brought you around? *(He slides closer to her.)*

MAURA. Well, I hope you don't think this is silly...

SCOTT. I'm ready for it.

MAURA. It was your posture.

SCOTT. Really?

MAURA. You see, you don't slouch. Most men slouch. I find slouching very unattractive and since you don't slouch I found that to be very....

SCOTT. Attractive?

MAURA. Uh...

SCOTT. Cool, hot? *(He tries to nuzzle her cheek.)*

MAURA. Actually, "agreeable" is still the best I can do.

(She rises and returns to the kitchen area.)

SCOTT. Well, I found you interesting right from the start.

MAURA. Did you? I don't know why? I didn't speak to anyone the entire day.

SCOTT. *(Rises.)* Which I found extremely interesting and somewhat provocative. In fact it was your whole demeanor. The conservative way you dress, wear your hair, very prim, very proper. You seem to be going out of your way to cover up your obvious attractiveness. That intrigued me. The longer the day went on, the more I wanted to know about you.

MAURA. Maybe you should have been concentrating a little more on the case.

SCOTT. I did my best. But my main focus seemed to be on you. And when I finally did approach you to ask you to dinner, I was scared to death you'd think I was just a wiseass who thought...maybe I shouldn't say this.

MAURA. You can't stop now. It wouldn't be fair.

SCOTT. Well, who thought you were just a loved–starved victim of the city who might be an easy mark.

MAURA. *(Slightly annoyed.)* Oh.

SCOTT. *(Worried.)* Have I offended you?

MAURA. Yes... But I'm taken by your honesty.

SCOTT. *(Relieved.)* I was hoping you would be. *(A beat.)* So, Maura, what else can I find out about you?

MAURA. Well, I did give you some information at dinner.

SCOTT. Yes, you did. But I'd really like to hear more. So far all I know is that you're originally from Iowa where you say you had a very normal, healthy childhood, which I find hard to believe about anyone born after 1970. That you've only lived in New York a couple of years and that you work for an apartment management firm which is how you got this great place and basically that's about it.

MAURA. And what you don't know but would like to know is?

SCOTT. The juicy side. The side that isn't so easy to talk about. The disappointments, the broken hearts...

MAURA. It's a little early in the acquaintance for that sort of information, isn't it?

SCOTT. Could be, but you'll find I'm very bad at small talk and to save both of us from certain boredom I suggest we get into the good stuff as soon as possible.

MAURA. Disappointments and broken hearts. Let's just say I had a few of each. How's that?

SCOTT. At best, underwhelming.

MAURA. Maybe I need to find out more about you before you find out more about me. So far I know that you're unattached, you've lived in New York for about ten years, and you're a stock analyst which I have no idea what that is but I find very impressive.

SCOTT. So did I, the first few years. I'm now thinking of going back to school for a teaching degree.

MAURA. A noble profession.

SCOTT. Involving a large pay cut and a lower standard of living but the more I think about it, the more I want to do it.

MAURA. Well, it's been said that if you really like what you do, you never work a day in your life.

SCOTT. I hope you're right. That would be like early retirement.

MAURA. And what about your juicy side?

SCOTT. Not that juicy. Two major love affairs. Two major failures.

MAURA. And the fault?

SCOTT. I seemed to have had unrealistic expectations. I wanted to live happily ever after and the other parties didn't think that was enough. I know it doesn't sound like a macho thing to admit to, but I don't really like being alone in this town. What about you?

(During the following **MAURA** *brings two cups of coffee to the coffee table.)*

MAURA. I think I've learned to deal with it and as time goes on, I'm starting to think I may prefer it.

SCOTT. Really?

MAURA. It seems so.

SCOTT. Wouldn't it be nice if I could be the guy to change that.

MAURA. Maybe. *(She sets the coffee cups down on the coffee table.)* Here we are. Do you take cream and sugar?

SCOTT. Neither.

*(***MAURA*** finds her self face to face with* **SCOTT.** *Suddenly the lights change giving us a bright, surreal look.* **SCOTT** *draws* **MAURA** *close to him and kisses her. There is no resistance on her part.)*

SCOTT. Was that okay?

MAURA. Yes. Yes, it was okay.

SCOTT. You said that like you're not sure.

MAURA. I'm not.

SCOTT. You're really determined not to let anyone in, aren't you?

MAURA. I'm not sure I can anymore.

SCOTT. Is it okay if I try?

MAURA. Why?

SCOTT. Because I'd like to.

MAURA. It never seems to work out.

SCOTT. Maybe this time it will. Maybe when you trust me enough.

MAURA. Maybe.

SCOTT. You will trust me, Maura. I promise you, you will.

(The lights return to normal. **SCOTT** *is totally unaware of the previous scene.* **MAURA** *composes herself. The two sit and begin to drink their coffee.)*

MAURA. Actually I'm glad I invited you up. I'm so wound up by this trial that I have a feeling I'm going to be awake all night anyway thinking about it.

SCOTT. I'm amazed I'm even serving jury duty. I've always been able to get out of it quite easily. But in this instance, for some strange reason, I felt it was about time I did my civic duty. And look how nicely it turned out. I met you.

MAURA. I'm very surprised to be on this case. I had read about it several months ago and now to be part of it, well, it's sort of surreal. God, the gruesome way he killed her ...

SCOTT. Allegedly killed her. The state has to prove it first, remember?

MAURA. I don't think that will be very difficult, do you? Just from the prosecuting attorney's opening remarks it seems he has more than enough evidence to convict that animal.

SCOTT. Well, that's up to us to judge isn't it? I mean that's what we're there for and I really think it's far too early and actually unfair to draw any definite conclusion until we've heard all the evidence and testimonies. In fact, if you remember, we were told very sternly by the judge that we weren't even to discuss the case among ourselves, not until we start deliberating the verdict.

MAURA. Yes. I'm sorry. You're absolutely right and up until now we haven't, although I have to admit it was extremely difficult not to talk about it at dinner. I'm not even sure we should even be together.

SCOTT. Well, none of the instructions the judge gave us said we couldn't be.

MAURA. We could ask him.

SCOTT. I guess we could. But I'd rather not. What if he thinks it's not a good idea? I wouldn't be able to take you to dinner tomorrow night and I've got my heart set on it.

MAURA. You're joking?

SCOTT. Not at all. I really enjoy your company and I have a feeling you sort of enjoy mine. I mean how many "agreeable" people do you meet in New York? What do you say?

MAURA. *(Rising.)* Yes, well, let me think about it for a while. I don't want to seem too anxious or desperate or pathetic, which is the way it might seem if 1 accepted your offer so readily. On the other hand, I'm not the kind of person to play games.

SCOTT. *(Rises.)* No. I didn't think you were.

MAURA. You don't think we're rushing things a bit?

SCOTT. We might be. But that could make things even more exciting. So, is it a "yes" for tomorrow night?

MAURA. Yes.

SCOTT. You've made me a happy man.

MAURA. Have I?

SCOTT. Extremely happy.

(They now face each other. SCOTT *draws her close to him and kisses her. This is a repeat of the earlier kissing scene except this time there is no change in the lighting.)*

SCOTT. *(Continuing, looks at her inquisitively.)* Was that okay?

MAURA. Yes. Yes, it was okay.

SCOTT. You said that like you're not sure.

MAURA. I'm not.

SCOTT. You're really determined not to let anyone in, aren't you?

MAURA. I'm not sure 1 can anymore.

SCOTT. Is it okay if I try?

MAURA. Why?

SCOTT. Because I'd like to.

MAURA. It never seems to work out.

SCOTT. Maybe this time it will. Maybe when you trust me enough.

MAURA. Maybe.

SCOTT. You will trust me, Maura. I promise you, you will.

MAURA. I hope so. I really want to.

SCOTT. You will.

(He kisses her again. Suddenly the lights dim. A bright, surreal light focuses on the door. While **SCOTT** *remains oblivious to this event,* **MAURA** *turns to the door as it opens.* **TOM** *and* **JAN**, *a couple about the same age as* **MAURA** *and* **SCOTT** *enter the apartment.)*

JAN. Oh, my. This is quite lovely.

TOM. I'm glad you like it. Like I said it's only one room but it has everything I need.

JAN. Oh I do like it. I like it a lot.

TOM. Yes. Everyone seems to. Everyone who's seen it. Actually not many people have. I'm not much on entertaining even though the room is quite conducive to it.

JAN. I feel very privileged.

TOM. The truth is, I'm really a very private person.

JAN. I more or less sensed that at dinner.

TOM. Did you? Good.

JAN. Oh, you've got a balcony. How lovely.

TOM. Yes. Would you like to take a look? *(Opens the balcony door.)*

JAN. I'd love to.

(They go out on the balcony. TOM closes the door behind them. The surreal light fades as JAN and TOM disappear into the darkness. Normal lighting focusing on MAURA and SCOTT comes up.)

SCOTT. I want this to work out between us, Maura. I really do.

MAURA. Yes, that would be nice. That would be very, very nice.

(SCOTT pulls MAURA to him and kisses her again as the stage fades to black.)

Scene 2

(The next day, early evening. The front door opens and **MAURA** *and* **SCOTT** *enter.* **SCOTT** *carries a bag of groceries that contain take-out food.* **MAURA** *turns on the lights and takes the bag from* **SCOTT**.*)*

SCOTT. I'm really glad we decided to bring food up. After sitting all day long in that courtroom, I'm not sure I could have handled sitting in a restaurant for any length of time.

MAURA. I don't remember ever being so drained.

(Opens kitchen doors, places bag on the counter and begins removillg containers of food and a bottle of wine.)

SCOTT. I did everything I could to keep from nodding off.

MAURA. Really? I don't know why. I found the day absolutely riveting.

SCOTT. My fatigue was not from the trial. It came from being awakened at three in the morning and told to go home.

MAURA. Well, I knew you wouldn't want to show tp in court wearing the exact same clothes you had on the day before. We certainly don't want to start anyone talking. Maybe after we adjourned you should have gone straight home and to bed.

SCOTT. How could I do that? If you recall, I had a hot date tonight. Actually, I'm starting to get a second wind. *(From behind he tries to nuzzle his cheek against hers.)* It could be from being close to you.

MAURA. That's sweet. *(***MAURA** *moves away, continuing to set up their dinner on the coffee table.)* You know what I find most fascinating about this trial? Stanway himself. His utter lack of emotions. He just sits there expressionless. Even during the detailed and gory way the prosecuting attorney described how he killed her.

SCOTT. Allegedly killed her.

MAURA. Yes, okay. Allegedly killed her. Anyway, I would think that if he really was innocent, this ordeal he's now going through would have to be a total nightmare for him. If he really was innocent you'd think there would be some expression of indignation or horror during the relating of the incident. My God, his wife is horribly bludgeoned to death and every time it's brought up, he just sits there showing absolutely nothing. No outrage, no pain, no grief, nothing. I find it almost impossible to believe that this is the behavior of an innocent man.

SCOTT. Time is a great healer. Don't forget he's been under arrest and awaiting trial for several months. I'm sure he's well aware of all the gory details and he's probably already dealt with that. Maybe if he was guilty he would put on the kind of show you think he should put on.

MAURA. I guess I'm not convinced he's at all remorseful. If I were in his shoes I would find this detached attitude very difficult to maintain no matter how much time has passed.

SCOTT. Fortunately I've never met a murderer so I wouldn't know how they behave or what goes through their minds. What about you? Have you ever met a murderer?

MAURA. Met one? No. Not that I know of. Anyway, what's the point you're trying to make?

SCOTT. No point. I'm just trying to get you to take a deep breath and chill out a little. There's still a lot that needs to be revealed about the case. It's just the second day. No one needs to come to any decision now. There's plenty of time.

MAURA. I know, you're right.

SCOTT. Thank you.

MAURA. But I also know I'm right about him doing it. I'll tell you what I also found fascinating. That so many of his friends were so willing to testify against him.

SCOTT. They weren't really testifying against him. They were simply verifying what seemed to be common knowledge, that his wife had a lover and he wasn't very happy about it.

MAURA. *(As she goes about dishing out food into plates.)* Pointing to all the reasons for his killing her. Jealousy, rage, betrayal.

SCOTT. My God, you've all but picked out the date this poor guy goes to the gas chamber, haven't you?

MAURA. No. Of course not. I said I could be fair and I will be. I'm simply going over what I was impressed by.

SCOTT. They also said that he was very much ill love with her. Desperately in love with her.

MAURA. Which only adds fuel to the fire.

SCOTT. Pointing to a crime of passion if anything.

MAURA. What ever the reason was, it's still murder. God, I still feel sick when I think of the photos they made us look at. Her skull smashed to bits by that brick and all that blood. All that horrible blood. You want to open the wine? There's a corkscrew in the desk drawer.

SCOTT. Oh, sure.

(**MAURA** *sets out two wine glasses on the coffee table. During the following* **SCOTT** *goes to the desk.)*

SCOTT. *(Continuing.)* That bothered me. Why a brick? He owned a gun. And there were plenty of knives around the house. Why a brick that obviously came from outside the house?

MAURA. I don't think it's necessary for us to concern ourselves over the way he chose to kill her. Our job is simply a case of did he or didn't he and unfortunately I think he did.

SCOTT. I know. But it just seems too easy. I mean if a guy is going to kill someone and then plead innocent, why would he make it so easy to convict him?

MAURA. That's true. On the other hand, it's probably the first time he's killed someone. Maybe next time he'll be more professional.

(**SCOTT** *turns to her. They look at each other for a beat.*)

SCOTT. You're cute, you know that? You are very very cute… when you let yourself be.

MAURA. Am I?

SCOTT. Very. (*He is about to open the desk drawer when a folder on top of the desk catches his eye. He picks it up and opens it*) What's this? "The Stanway Case." You're keeping a file?

MAURA. (*Going to him.*) Well, I'm just starting to. I was hoping the case might make a good book. Possibly even a play. At this point I'm not exactly sure.

SCOTT. You're a writer?

MAURA. I'd like to think I am. That's another reason why I came to New York. It seems unless you've spent some time on the east coast, no one really takes what you write very seriously.

SCOTT. Then you've been published?

MAURA. Well, no, not yet, which is a little troubling because I'm not sure it's really ethical to call oneself a writer until one's been published. It's a bit of a thin line.

SCOTT. Well, maybe this Stanway case will do the trick. (*Leafs through pages.*) You've already got a bunch of notes. I'm impressed, especially since it's only the second day of the trial. When did you find time to start this?

MAURA. Early this morning. After you left. I jotted down some things that I thought were important. Anyway, it's not for anyone's eyes yet.

(*Taking the folder from* **SCOTT**, *she places it in a desk arawer.*)

SCOTT. You've got to promise to let me read it when you finish, although I guess I'll know how it ends, won't I?

MAURA. Maybe. (*She then takes out the corkscrew from the desk drawer and hands it to Scott.*) Here you are. The corkscrew. I don't know why I keep it in the desk.

SCOTT. Why not? It's near the wine rack. It makes sense.

(*He takes the bottle of wine from the kitchen counter and opens it.*)

SCOTT. *(Continuing.)* Anyway, let's forget the case tonight, okay? Let's talk about other things. Let's talk about last night. It was pretty amazing, wasn't it? I mean for me, anyway. How was it for you? I know this is a little late to be asking that but better late than never. By the way, is that part going to be in your book? It could help sales.

(He puts the corkscrew back in the drawer, crosses to coffee table and pours two glasses of wine.)

MAURA. *(A beat.)* I admire you. I really do. You are approaching this trial in such a fair and logical manner. And in the end I suppose I will too, but right now, cut and dry, the best I can say is Stanway is guilty as sin. *(She returns to sofa)*

SCOTT. You don't give an inch, do you?

MAURA. At times I have been accused of having somewhat of a stubborn streak.

SCOTT. Look, what if we make a pact, put it in writing and sign it? When we leave the jury room, we leave the case there too. Does that sound reasonable?

MAURA. You are asking me to suppress my feelings.

SCOTT. *(Sits next to MAURA.)* I'm asking you to obey the judge and the law. I think at the end of the day we need to leave it all in the courtroom.

MAURA. It seems I'm obviously much more affected by this trial than you. Maybe it's because I'm a woman. We seem to be more sensitive in some areas than our male counterparts.

SCOTT. Come on, Maura. You know just as well as I do that's pure bullshit.

MAURA. Well, I think we do.

SCOTT. *(Slightly irritated.)* Think, think, think. Maybe that's your problem. Maybe you need to concentrate on what you hear, not what you think.

MAURA. *(Playfully.)* Okay, I'll buy that and so far everything I've heard seems to point to him and I doubt very much that he's going to get away with it and I don't see how anyone on that jury in their right mind can see it any other way.

SCOTT. God, you're a friggin' handful, aren't you" *(Hands a wine glass to* **MAURA** *and then offers a toast.)* Well, here's to us.

MAURA. No. "To you and me," please. I'm not ready for "us" just yet.

SCOTT. Will that make you more comfortable?

MAURA. For now it would.

SCOTT. "To you and me."

(The lighting changes to surreal.)

MAURA. *(Rising, upset.)* I need to know where you stand, Scott. I need to know why the hell you even think there's a possibility that Stanway didn't do it. Trust me. He's an abusive, controlling pig. I know that kind of man. He would rather see his wife dead than lose her. I... I can't talk to you about this anymore. Maybe I need to be alone.

SCOTT. Look, get a grip. We've got something special here, you and I. Why can't you see that? I want to keep this relationship going and no matter what you say it is now a relationship.

MAURA. No it isn't. At best it's an affair and frankly one I'd now like to reconsider.

*(***MAURA** *sits. She regains her composure. The lighting changes back to normal.* **SCOTT** *is unaware of the surreal moment.)*

SCOTT. *(Repeating his toast.)* "To you and me."

(They clink glasses together and drink.)

MAURA. What did you mean when you said I'm cute when I let myself be?

SCOTT. I meant that you have the ability to be very cute, actually bordering on adorable, when you let your guard down a bit. When you don't seem to be... hiding things.

MAURA. Hiding things? How did you arrive at that? I think I've been very open.

SCOTT. Yes. About the case. But other than that you just seem so damn cautious about everything else. I feel you've built some kind of a wall around you and I'm wondering at what point do I get let in because I'd really like to be.

MAURA. Yes.!...I know that.

SCOTT. Maybe after the trial. Maybe that's when you'll feel more at ease with our situation. God, even today in court, you seemed to go out of your way to avoid any hint of intimacy between us. You wouldn't sit next to me at lunch and every break we took you seemed to disappear somewhere. Actually, I felt a little rejected.

(They begin to eat.)

MAURA. I'm sorry but I didn't want anyone getting any ideas.

SCOTT. That we're involved with one another? I don't see anything wrong with that since the fact seems to be that we are.

MAURA. Well, it doesn't seem appropriate, I mean not so soon.

SCOTT. I think that's the magic of the situation. That it was so soon. And the fact that I'm here for a second night and drinking wine, that should tell you something. Besides, I would hate knowing I was nothing more than a one-night stand. You're not sorry about last night, are you?

MAURA. Maybe a little.

SCOTT. ah.

MAURA. Actually, a lot.

SCOTT. Because we had sex on our first night?

MAURA. It's not something a woman is usually proud of.

SCOTT. Yes, but on the other hand it's something a man is, so the two things sort of balance each other out. Anyway, if you want some sort of stronger commitment on my part, I'm more than willing.

MAURA. No. I don't need that.

SCOTT. Maybe I do.

MAURA. Look, it's much too soon to make what happened last night more important than what it was.

SCOTT. And what do you think it was?

MAURA. It was simply two people who didn't want to be alone at that particular point in time.

SCOTT. You need to know this about me, Maura. I'm very self sufficient when I need to be. I have no trouble spending my nights alone even though I don't particularly like it. I wanted to be with you because I wanted to be with you. It had nothing to do with not wanting to be alone or just wanting to have sex. It was strictly you, Maura. I wanted to be with you.

MAURA. Scott, doesn't it bother you that I seem to be acting so unreasonable about Stanway?

SCOTT. It concerns me. It doesn't bother me.

MAURA. He did kill her, you know. He definitely did kill her.

SCOTT. So what?

(*He kisses her. The lights fade out on them. Surreal lighting comes up as* **TOM** *and* **JAN** *re-renter from the balcony.*)

JAN. I absolutely love this place.

TOM. It's extremely bright and cheerful in the daytime and at night quite cozy and somewhat formal for a studio apartment.

JAN. It's very Parisian.

TOM. Have you been to Paris?

JAN. No. Not yet. But one day I hope to go.

TOM. You should. You'd find it very agreeable.

JAN. Agreeable. I like that word. It's not used very often.

TOM. I know.

JAN. (*She notices a manuscript on the desk. She picks it up curiously.*) The Stanway Case? I remember that one. Lawrence Stanway, the real estate guy. Didn't he murder his wife?

TOM. Some people thought so. I felt there'd be a good book in it. Or at the very least a play.

JAN. You're a writer?

TOM. Well, somewhat. I haven't been published or produced yet. I was hoping this project might do it. How about a glass of wine?

JAN. Yes, I'd like one.

TOM. Red or white?

(He gets a couple of glasses.)

JAN. It doesn't matter. Either would be fine.

(TOM takes a bottle of red wine from the wine rack and looks at her.)

TOM. I feel it's a red kind of night. Red has more tone. Seems to set a better mood.

JAN. For what?

TOM. For a lot of things. Romance. Mystery. Intrigue.

(JAN opens the drawer and takes out the corkscrew and hands it to him.)

JAN. Good. Let's have red then. Here's the corkscrew.

TOM. *(Thrown. A beat.)* How did you know it was in that drawer?

JAN. I... I don't know. That's strange. It was kind of a normal reflex. I just went there and got it. But I don't know why.

TOM. *(Takes the corkscrew and opens wine.)* It's this apartment. One of the jurors actually lived here. That's one of the reasons I rented it. It had an aura about it. A disturbing one. Like it knew something. Something bad... Something unpleasant.

JAN. Oh, my. I just felt a chill. Really kind of a creepy one.

TOM. Good. I mean good in a creative sense. *(He pours the wine and hands her a glass.)* Well, "here's to us" unless of course you prefer "here's to you and me."

JAN. Why don't I let you decide.

TOM. "To us!"

(They lift their glasses, then sip their wine)

TOM. *(Continuing.)* Maybe you'd like to read what I've written on The Stanway case.

JAN. Yes, I'd love to.

TOM. I knew you would.

*(**TOM** takes the manuscript from the desk and hands it to her. As she takes it he kisses her. He meets no resistance.)*

TOM. *(Continuing.)* Was that okay?

JAN. *(Uncertain.)* Yes. Yes, it was okay.

TOM. You said that like you're not sure.

JAN. For some reason... I'm not.

TOM. Maybe when you trust me enough. Basically, trust is what it's all about.

*(**JAN** and **TOM** remain in their places as the surreal lights dim on them and normal lighting comes up on **MAURA** and **SCOTT**.)*

SCOTT. I've been waiting for someone like you to come into my life for a long time, Maura. A long, long time.

(The lights fade to black.)

Scene 3

(Several evenings later. We hear the key in the lock. The apartment door bursts open and **MAURA** *enters closing the door behind her. She switches on the light. She is visibly upset. She goes to her desk and removes the folder from the drawer. She sits and begins to make some notations. The doorbell rings.* **MAURA** *just looks at the door and doesn't move. It rings again. Still, she does nothing. Then there is heavy knocking on the door.)*

SCOTT. *(offstage)* Maura! Maura. I know you're in there.

*(***MAURA*** puts the folder back in the drawer and reluctantly goes to the door and lets Scott in.)*

SCOTT. *(Continuing.)* Why did you do that? Why did you run off the way you did?

MAURA. I needed to go home.

SCOTT. To go home or to get away from me?

MAURA. I'll let you choose the answer.

SCOTT. Six words, Maura. That's all there were between us. Six words. One from you and five from me and you react like I just blew up the world.

MAURA. I don't want to discuss it. Not now.

SCOTT. Well damn it, I do. I'm not going to let it intensify into something more than it is. Damn it, six stupid words and you go sailing off like a lunatic. You said, "Well?" And I said "I need to hear more" and the next thing I know you're in a cab and gone.

MAURA. If that was Stanway's wife instead of Stanway on trial, you'd have a whole different attitude. Admit it. You know damn well you would.

SCOTT. *(Incredulous.)* Ah, please. Give me a break. Are you accusing me of being a woman hater? Is that it? You couldn't be more wrong. Look how I've been putting up with you.

MAURA. I found your dark side, Scott. I knew it was there and now it's coming out.

SCOTT. I thought we decided not to talk about the trial anymore until we begin deliberation.

MAURA. There was no agreement. I said I would do my best and I am. Unfortunately you being blind to the truth makes the situation a lot more difficult.

SCOTT. What the hell is your goddamn rush to convict this guy? If he's going down, he'll go down. Come on, maybe I made a mistake. Maybe I should have said "I'd like to hear more" instead of "I need to hear more." Would that have made a difference?

MAURA. You heard the coroner's report. The brick she was killed with had his DNA on it. And there was mud on his shoes from the garden. How much more proof do you need?

SCOTT. It all fits in with the statement Stanway gave to the police when they arrived on the scene. He said he was out in the garden when he heard her scream. As far as his DNA on the brick, he said he found the brick lying outside their bedroom and instinctively picked it up to use in case he needed to defend himself. He had no idea it was used to kill his wife. It all makes sense to me but for some reason you just want to ignore those facts.

MAURA. Facts! It's a killer's lame alibi. There wasn't a trace of anyone else being in that room but him.

SCOTT. It's too pat. Too perfect. Something doesn't seem right.

MAURA. Yes, and at this point I think it's you. I think you want him to go free. You plan for him to go free.

SCOTT. Where the hell are you coming from? Do you think I'm a plant? That I've been put on the jury to protect Stanway?

MAURA. We need twelve people to convict him. It's obvious you seem to be the only one not getting it.

SCOTT. How do you know what anyone gets or doesn't get? I've never seen you talk to anyone.

MAURA. You pick up vibes.

SCOTT. Vibes? Great. Send a guy to the gas chamber on vibes. Welcome to the 21st century, Maura. We're supposed to be dealing with facts, not vibes.

MAURA. The facts are that he was abusive both mentally and physically. We heard testimony of that nature from several witnesses.

SCOTT. He loved her, Maura. Why can't you get that through your head? That has to carry some weight and right now it does with me.

MAURA. Oh, really? Have you forgotten the O.J. case? I'm sorry, Scott, if we are so wide apart on this, God knows how wide apart we are on other things.

SCOTT. You know something, Maura. You're a goddamn bully.

MAURA. Well, maybe it's a good thing you found that out now.

SCOTT. Well, lucky for you I happen to like bullies. They're terrific in bed.

MAURA. *(Slaps him.)* I don't find that amusing. I really don't.

SCOTT. *(Takes a moment or two to recover. He takes a deep breath.)* It's a good thing we haven't talked politics. I'd hate to think what would happen if you were a Democrat and I was a Republican.

MAURA. *(Emphatically.)* I am a Democrat.

SCOTT. *(Disgusted.)* That's just great. *(A beat.)* Maybe we both could use a glass of wine.

MAURA. No thank you.

SCOTT. Well, I need one.

(During the following **SCOTT** *gets the corkscrew from the desk and a bottle of wine from the wine rack and opens it. As he puts the corkscrew back in the desk drawer, something in the drawer catches his eye for a moment. He glances over at* **MAURA,** *who is not looking at him, and slips a key into his pocket. He then closes the desk drawer and pours a glass of wine for himself.)*

SCOTT. *(cont.)* Look, there are two parts to our involvement. The first part is you and me. The second part is you, me and this goddamn trial. They need to be kept separate.

MAURA. He did it, Scott. It's so obvious he did it. And the fact that you even think there's a possibility he didn't… I can't get past that. This case doesn't just define where each of us stands. It also defines who each of us is.

SCOTT. Think about what you're doing Maura. You're asking me to make a judgment before the trial is even over.

MAURA. I need to know where you stand, Scott. I need to know why the hell you even think there's a possibility that Stanway didn't do it. Trust me. He's an abusive, controlling pig. I know that kind of man. He would rather see his wife dead than lose her. I…I can't talk to you about this any more. Maybe I need to be alone.

SCOTT. Look, get a grip! We've got something good here, you and I. Why can't you see that? I want to keep this relationship going and no matter what you say it is now a relationship.

MAURA. No it isn't. At best it's an affair and frankly one I'd now like to reconsider.

SCOTT. *(Trying to regain a calmness.)* Come on, Maura. Up until now these past few days have been the best days of my life. And I think they've been pretty terrific for you too. We need to hang in. Look, the trial can't last any longer than a couple more days. There are just a few more testimonies we need to hear and then we deliberate and you can yell and scream your head off at me all you want. But not here and not now because it's really starting to get to me.

MAURA. Then leave.

SCOTT. No. Not like this. We need to calm down. Both of us.

MAURA. You know he's not taking the stand.

SCOTT. So?

MAURA. You don't think that proves something?

SCOTT. No. Yes. I don't know. A lot of defendants don't take the stand.

MAURA. And how many who don't do you think are innocent?

SCOTT. I don't know. Maybe some of them. Maybe none of them. I don't know. All I know is that this trial has affected you in a very unhealthy way and I'm having a hard time dealing with it.

MAURA. Please go home.

SCOTT. No! Not yet! What the hell is your overwhelming need to fry this guy? Don't you see what you're doing? You are letting this stupid trial destroy something that neither of us may ever find again. Maybe we need to excuse ourselves from the jury. There are several jury alternates. They can just put two of those guys in. I'll talk to the judge in the morning.

MAURA. No. No. I need to see this through.

SCOTT. Why? I don't understand you! There's something you're not telling me, isn't there? Something you don't want me to know. There is, isn't there?

MAURA. *(A long beat. She has a difficult time divulging this information.)* What if I told you I saw him do it? What if I told you I saw him pick up the brick and kill her. I saw him take lhe brick and beat her head into a bloody pulp.

SCOTT. You saw?

MAURA. I saw him do it, Scott. I did. You see… I get…I get visions.

SCOTT. *(Disbelief)* Oh, shit.

MADRA. I know you don't believe me, but so help me it's true. I get visions. It's not an easy thing to live with. Some are visions of things that have happened. Some are visions of things that will happen.

SCOTT. *(Holding his wine glass up and looking to the sky.)* Do I pick 'em. Do I know how to pick 'em.

MAURA. You don't believe me, do you?

SCOTT. I believe you're having some kind of a meltdown and we'd better do something about it right away.

MAURA. Good night, Scott. Just go home.

SCOTT. Don't send me away, Maura. Not tonight. You need to be with somebody.

(He tries to hold her. She turns away)

MAURA. Maybe I do, but obviously not with you.

SCOTT. Please, Maura. We need to hold on. Don't you understand? You mean something to me. There's nothing I want more than to make you part of my world.

MAURA. *(Taunting.)* Part of your world? Like territory, right? Just like Stanway's wife was to him. I think it's getting to be pretty clear what your world is and no thank you.

SCOTT. Damn it! Are you going to put everything I say now under a microscope? You know perfectly well what I mean.

MAURA. Go home, Scott. I'm not in the mood for this or you.

SCOTT. In just a few days you've become a different person. A person I don't know. I want that first person I met back, Maura. She was sweet and she was kind and I want her back because I loved her and she loved me.

MAURA. Loved you? What the hell are you talking about? I never ever said I loved you. Look, go home. I need to be alone. I mean it! Go home!

SCOTT. *(Hurt and threatening.)* She loved me, Maura, trust me. That person that was you loved me and I want her back. And I'll tell you something else. I'm going to get her back. You'll see. *(Gulps down his drink, puts the glass down, and then points at her)* I'm going to get her back.

(He exits. She locks the door, stands with her back leaning against it for a moment and then crosses to the desk. The surrea lights come up. MAURA *turns and gasps as the front door opens and* JAN *and* TOM *enter.* TOM

carries a bag of groceries. **MAURA** *watches and reacts to the scene.)*

TOM. I'm really glad we decided to eat in. Actually, I really wanted you to come up tonight for sort of a selfish reason.

JAN. I have to be honest. I sort of suspected that.

TOM. *(Opens kitchen doors and places bag on counter.)* I want you to read the rest of my pages on the Stanway case.

JAN. That was not what I suspected.

TOM. Well, unless you were being polite you said you were fairly intrigued by what you've read so far. I'd like very much to hear what you think of the rest of it.

JAN. I don't know why. I'm not much of a reader or a critic.

TOM. Well, fortunately you don't have to be one to be the other. The truth is, Jan, you've become very important to me.

JAN. I have? So quickly?

TOM. I have a good feeling about us. There's nothing I would like more than to make you part of my world.

(He starts towards the desk.)

MAURA. *(To* **TOM***)* What?

TOM. *(Turning to* **MAURA***.)* I said I would like to make her part of my world. Are you having a problem with that?

MAURA. Oh, my God.

(As **TOM** *goes to desk and gets his manuscript for* **JAN***,* **MAURA** *rushes to* **JAN***'s side.* **JAN** *is oblivious to her.)*

MAURA. *(Continuing.)* Look, you've got to get out of here. You've got to get away from him.

JAN. *(To* **TOM***.)* Part of your world? That's very sweet but we barely know one another. Actually it's only our second date.

*(***TOM** *opens the manuscript to the new pages and hands it to* **JAN***.)*

TOM. Sometimes that's all it takes. Here. Read these. Tell me what you think.

MAURA. *(Desperately pleading.)* Listen to me! You need to get out of here! Now! Please! You need to get out!

*(***TOM*** smiles, knowing **MAURA***'s plea is useless. The surreal lights slowly fade to black. The light on* **MAURA** *becomes a spot and then also fades to black)*

END OF ACT I

ACT TWO

Scene 1

*(Late Afternoon. **MAURA**, in a funk, is sitting on the sofa in her bathrobe and eating yogurt from the carton. **JAN**, sitting in the same chair as in the previous scene, is reading the manuscript. **TOM** is seated at the desk and writing on a pad of paper. Surrealn lighting is on all three. After a few beats **JAN** lowers the manuscript and turns to **TOM**.)*

JAN. She gets visions?

TOM. Yes. *(He puts the pad in the desk drawer.)*

JAN. I'm having a hard time with that.

TOM. Really?

JAN. Yes. I thought this story was based on a real situation.

TOM. *(He sits on the arm of the sofa near her chair.)* It is.

JAN. Oh, come on.

TOM. You don't buy it?

JAN. Not at all. I mean the case itself makes sense and your approach is good. A guy murders his wife. We follow two jurors with opposing viewpoints. Yeah, that's fine. But the visions. I think that's where you lose me. Unless you've decided to go the Stephen King route. You know, that supernatural genre. If that's where you're headed, then I might buy into it. Reluctantly, of course, because that's not what I expected and frankly I don't really care for that sort of stuff. I find it a total copout for good old fashioned, down-to-earth behavior.

TOM. You don't think people get visions? Real people? Like you, like me? Who can see things that will happen, that can and do happen?

37

JAN. I'm sorry. Forgive me. I happen to be relatively logical. There is no Santa Claus, there are no vampires, and people in real life don't get visions. And this juror, if she really does exist...

MAURA. *(To* JAN.*)* I do. I do exist.

JAN. *(Not acknowledging* MAURA.*)* Well, she has got to be a total loony.

MAURA. But I'm not. I'm not a loony and I do get visions.

JAN. I'll keep reading but I think you might be on thin ice.

*(*JAN *continues reading. The phone rings. The surreal lights dim on* JAN *and* TOM *and the normal lights come up on* MAURA *who approaches the answering machine and stares at it. On the fourth ring the answering machine picks up.)*

MAURA. *(V.O. on answering machine.)* This is Maura. I can't come to the phone now. Leave a message and I'll get back to you as soon as I can. *(The machine beeps for a reply.)*

SCOTT. *(V.O. on answering machine.)* Maura, this is Scott. I know you're there. Please answer the phone. It is so wrong of you to do this to me. I deserve better. Please, pick up the phone. It's a gorgeous Saturday afternoon and everyone's in the park. Maybe you and I might go out for a walk and...

(During the above MAURA *goes over to the phone, lifts it off the receiver and slams it down cutting off the message. The phone rings again. After four rings the answering machine picks up again.)*

MAURA. *(V.O. on answering machine.)* This is Maura. I can't come to the phone now. Leave a message and I'll get back to you as soon as I can. *(The machine beeps for a reply.)*

SCOTT. *(V.O. on answering machine.)* Goddamn it, Maura. Stop being a bitch. Look, I'm downstairs on my cell phone and I'm coming up. Please let me in. You are being absolutely unreasonable.

(The answering machine clicks off. **MAURA**, *finished with the yogurt, puts the container and the spoon in the sink. The doorbell rings followed by knocking.)*

SCOTT. *(O.S. continuing.)* Maura! Maura! Please, I need to talk to you.

*(***MAURA*** *enters the bathroom as* **SCOTT** *continues to knock on the door. The knocking becomes louder and more threatening.)*

SCOTT. *(O.S., continuing)* Maura!

(A beat and then we hear a key being inserted in the lock. **JAN** *and* **TOM**'s *area remains dim. Normal lights come up as* **SCOTT** *enters the apartment. A beat later* **MAURA** *comes out of the bathroom. They are face to face.* **MAURA** *is horrified.)*

MAURA. *(Shrieking.)* Oh, my God! How did you get in here?

SCOTT. Take it easy. Take it easy. I used a key.

MAURA. A key? How the hell did you ...

SCOTT. It was in your desk drawer. I saw it there the other night when I went to get the corkscrew. You've been behaving so irrational, talking so crazy, I was worried you might do something to yourself. I took the key just in case.

MAURA. Well, now that you see I'm okay, just put the key back on the desk and leave. Otherwise I'm calling the police.

SCOTT. I don't get you, Maura. I really don't get you.

MAURA. It doesn't matter because I get you and you have turned out to be one big jerk. And I'm not alone in my thoughts. Six days! We've been deliberating for six days and everyone thinks he's guilty but you. This trial should have been over and done with by now but you keep calling for the same evidence over and over. As if you're trying to find a loophole to prove him innocent.

SCOTT. It's because I'm not taking this case lightly. I've read and re-read all the transcripts and I have to tell you there are problems.

MAURA. There are no problems.

SCOTT. The jury totally ignored the testimony from Stanway's wife's best friend. That Stanway's wife was going to give up her lover and try and work things out with Stanway.

MAURA. Maybe she did. But we don't know at the time Stanway knew that.

SCOTT. It's also possible her lover could have killed her when she tried to break off with him.

MAURA. Oh, my God. Where are you getting this from? Wasn't it you who was so adamant about concentrating on what we hear, not what we think? Her lover was out of the country when she was killed.

SCOTT. He could have hired someone to do it for him. That's not out of the question.

MAURA. Why would he? He had no idea she was going back to her husband.

SCOTT. Well, maybe he had other motives. There are all kinds of possibilities when it comes to love. Anyway, Stanway has a right to a fair trial no matter how long it takes.

MAURA. You are such an ignoramus. You're forgetting the most important thing. I told you, I saw him do it!

SCOTT. Sure. Tell anyone else that and they'll lock you up quicker than they'll lock up Stanway.

MAURA. This trial is about you now, isn't it Scott? You've got eleven people trying to convince you Stanway's guilty but you can't bring yourself to accept it because it's really your guilt that's on trial?

SCOTT. That's nuts. That's absolutely nuts.

MAURA. You identify with Stanway. Pure and simple. By declaring him innocent you think it lets you off the hook.

SCOTT. I can't believe this.

MAURA. You identify with him and I can only guess why. Most likely that you too are an abusive piece of crap. Is that why those other women left you?

SCOTT. I'd stop it now. I'd stop it right now.

MAURA. I hit on it, didn't I, Scott? You and Stanway. Two peas in a pod.

SCOTT. *(Loud. Threatening. He comes closer to her.)* I said I'd stop it right now! *(Takes a deep breath and backs off)* Look, I find it very embarrassing the way you're ignoring me. People are sensing something's wrong between us and I'd like to not have their eyes on me as much as they are. So until the case is over, at least try not to be so... so distant.

MAURA. You didn't tell anyone that we...

SCOTT. Slept together? Having an affair? Why? Are you ashamed? Look, I'm in love with you. Or at least was in love with you. I'm not even sure myself anymore because you've got my head so screwed up I don't know what the hell I am anymore. I had hoped that you were in love with me and I guess I wanted other people to know about it. *(Sits on sofa.)*

MAURA. You are one needy bastard, aren't you?

SCOTT. Yes. And I needed you.

MAURA. Just give me my key, Scott, and go. For your own good, please, go.

(The surreal lighting comes up on them.)

SCOTT. *(Confused.)* I...I can't. I can't move.

MAURA. I tried to warn you, Scott. I tried to get you to back off. I really did.

SCOTT. My body. I can't... I can't feel it.

MAURA. Poor Scott. Poor, poor Scott.

(Surreal lights out. Normal lights in.)

MAURA. *(Continuing.)* Please go, Scott. I mean it.

SCOTT. *(Rising.)* It's this asinine trial. That's why it isn't working out between us. Once it's over I know you'll feel differently.

MAURA. Don't you get it? Once it's over I never want to see you again.

SCOTT. You little bitch.

(**SCOTT** *slaps her. She falls back onto the sofa.*)

SCOTT. *(Continuing.)* You make loving you very difficult, Maura. Very difficult!

(*The lights dim on* **MAURA** *and* **SCOTT** *and the surreal lights come up on* **TOM** *and* **JAN**.)

JAN. I'm sorry, Tom. This is now making me very nervous. I don't like where it's going. I'm not enjoying it at all now.

TOM. Relax. You've only got a few pages left.

JAN. They both seemed so nice and pleasant at the beginning. It could have been a sweet romance or a charming comedy. And then you made them sicker and sicker…

TOM. Wait a minute. I didn't make them anything. They are what they are.

JAN. You're the writer.

TOM. Yes, but they're the people.

JAN. Well, they're creepy and dreadfully unstable and you need to fix them.

TOM. But then they won't be who they are.

JAN. So what? It's a debatable point anyway. I am uncomfortable being around them and I'm starting to become uncomfortable being around you.

TOM. Are you?

JAN. I am.

TOM. Look, read a little more and then we'll talk about it. Please… Please?

(**JAN** *looks at him, sighs, and continues reading. The surreal lights go out. Normal lights go back on* **SCOTT** *and* **MAURA**. **SCOTT** *tries to put his arms around* **MAURA**, *who holds her pained cheek.*)

SCOTT. I'm sorry, Maura. I'm so sorry.

MAURA. *(She pushes him away as violently as she can.)* Don't touch me. Just don't touch me.

SCOTT. You made me do that, you know. I didn't want to hit you but you pushed too far. You know you did.

MAURA. I was so right about you. You and Stanway. You're one and the same, aren't you?

SCOTT. No. No, we're not! The last thing I want to do is hurt you. I never wanted to hurt anyone. How many times do I have to tell you I love you? In spite of your unreasonable behavior towards me, I still love you. Why can't you see that?

(He tries to hold her. She backs away.)

MAURA. You don't know who you're screwing with, you bastard. You haven't got a clue. Now get out! Just get out!

SCOTT. Please, Maura…

MAURA. *(Screaming.)* Get out and leave me alone. I never want to see you again. Go! And give me my key.

*(**SCOTT** flings the key against the wall and points at **MAURA** menacingly.)*

SCOTT. I could kill you. For what you're doing to me, I could kill you.

MAURA. I'll bet you could.

*(**SCOTT** exits, slamming the door behind him. Lights fade on **MAURA** as she enters the bathroom, closing the door behind her. Surreal lighting on **TOM** and **JAN**.)*

JAN. *(Rising.)* It's late. I need to go home.

TOM. But you haven't finished.

JAN. *(Crossing to door.)* No, I can't. I don't want to.

TOM. I'm asking you nicely.

JAN. No, I want to go. I don't want to be here anymore. *(Waves the manuscript at him.)* Not with these people… and truthfully, not with you… not anymore.

(She hands him the manuscript and opens the door. He slams it shut before she can leave.)

TOM. Then I'll have to ask you not so nicely.

(He begins to push her back towards the chair she was sitting in)

TOM. *(Cont.)* Finish the goddamn story. You're not leaving here until you do.

(*JAN sits.* **TOM** *shoves the manuscript at her. She takes it but doesn't return to reading it as quickly as* **TOM** *would like her to.*)

I mean it!

JAN. *(Angry.)* Okay. Okay. Just keep away from me.

TOM. I'm actually quite harmless.

JAN. If you were, you would have let me leave when I wanted to.

TOM. I would hate to have this evening put a damper on our relationship.

JAN. God, you are just as sick as the people you write about, aren't you?

TOM. Let me think about that. It could be a compliment. But then again, maybe not. You're frightened, aren't you?

JAN. Concerned.

TOM. For Maura or for Scott?

JAN. For me. Just promise that when I finish this I can leave.

TOM. You're cute, you know that? You are very, very cute... when you let yourself be.

JAN. Oh, shut up.

(*JAN continues reading. Surreal lights dim down on* **JAN** *and* **TOM.** *Normal light up on* **MAURA** *who comes out of the bathroom, dressed to travel. She goes to the closet and brings out two suitcases and sets them down in a prominent place. She returns to the closet. Surreal lights on* **JAN** *and* **TOM.** **TOM** *goes over and rubs* **JAN** *'s shoulders as she reads.*)

TOM. I'm sorry. I didn't mean to upset you.

JAN. Don't touch me. Just don't touch me.

(*Surreal lights go down. Normal lights up on* **MAURA** *as she comes out of the closet with a purse. A folded itinerary sticks out of the outside pocket. She closes the closet* *door and places the purse on the desk. The phone rings four times.)*

MAURA. *(V.O. on answering machine.)* This is Maura. I can't come to the phone now. Leave a message and I'll get back to you as soon as I can. *(The machine beeps for a reply)*

SCOTT. *(V.O. on answering machine.)* Goddamn it, Maura. Why won't you return my calls? It isn't fair, damn it. Now that the trial is over I know things will be different between us. Give me a chance, Maura. Give us both a chance. I'll do whatever you want to make this work. You saw that at the trial. I did exactly what you wanted me to do. Please, Maura. What you're doing to me isn't fair. It really isn't. I love you. I'm downstairs and I'm coming up.

*(***MAURA*** picks up the phone.)*

MAURA. Scott. You listen to me. You come up here and so help me I'll call the police. Scott! Scott!

*(He's not there. ***MAURA*** hangs up. The surreal lighting now comes up on ***TOM*** and ***JAN***.)*

MAURA. *(to ***TOM***.)* What now?

TOM. *(Nodding to ***MAURA***.)* You know perfectly well, what now. You have no choice.

JAN. *(To ***TOM***.)* You just put yourself in the story.

TOM. Did I? I hadn't noticed.

*(***TOM*** now enters ***MAURA***'s lighting whenever he desires. During the following ***MAURA*** goes to the bookshelf, reaches behind some books and removes a small vial. She looks at it intently.)*

JAN. You... You're insane, aren't you?

TOM. *(Angrily.)* Is that the only word you can come up with? Insane? Not imaginative? Not creative? God, I hate insane. I would have actually preferred demented or even deranged, rather than insane. Troubled wouldn't be bad either. My parents found me very troubled.

Some people say I killed them. Look, just finish reading the piece, damn it. Just finish. And if you haven't got anything nice to say then just don't say anything. *(Angrier.)* You got that?

JAN. *(Intimidated.)* Yes.

TOM. *(As he gets a bottle of wine, the corkscrew and a wine glass.)* God, some people are so difficult.

*(The surreal lights remain on **JAN** as she goes back to reading. The doorbell rings. **MAURA** ignores it. It rings again. **MAURA** continues to ignore it. Then there is pounding on the door.)*

SCOTT. *(offstage)* Damn it, Maura. I know you're in there. Let me in!

*(The door begins to shake violently from **SCOTT** trying to force it open.)*

MAURA. Go away Scott! If you know what's good for you, you'll go away!

SCOTT. *(offstage)* Please, Maura, Please. We need to talk.

MAURA. All right, I'm calling the police. I'll let them deal with you.

SCOTT. *(offstage)* You bitch! You goddamn bitch! As far as I'm concerned you can burn in hell.

(There is a loud kick at the door and then silence.)

TOM. You know he's not going to give up that easily.

MAURA. I know.

TOM. I wouldn't. Not if I cared as much about someone as he says he cares about you.

(He pours a glass of wine and sets it on the desk.)

MAURA. You know this is not what I wanted.

TOM. No, I don't. In fact I think this is exactly what you wanted.

MAURA. Do you? Then maybe it is.

*(She opens the vial and empties it into the glass of wine that **TOM** has poured.)*

JAN. *(Rising.)* She's going to poison him?

TOM. *(Angry.)* Goddamn it. Just finish reading and mind your own business. This doesn't concern you.

JAN. *(She goes to him with the manuscript.)* Now I see what you're doing. Your threats, your anger. You're trying to frighten me, aren't you? You'd like me to feel the fear that you want Maura to feel. You think you might not be able to do it with just these stupid pages so you're trying to intensify my feelings about your disgustingly repulsive story which I know now is a total fabrication.

TOM. You'd really like to believe that, wouldn't you? You'd like to believe that the world is actually a nice, safe, wonderful place where everyone acts rational and decent and there's no need to worry about anything or anyone.

JAN. No, no. I'm not that naïve. I know there's plenty of bad, but there's also lots of good. Why can't you look at the good part? Why do you have to concentrate on the sinister, the menacing? Why did you have to make everyone so twisted and depraved?

TOM. For the last time, I'm telling you I didn't make them anything that they weren't. This is what they were and this is what they did. I'm just a writer putting it down the way this apartment told me to.

JAN. It told you to? This apartment told you to? Oh, my God, you are even sicker than....

(Suddenly SCOTT *bursts through the French doors.* JAN *screams in horror. Even* TOM *is surprised and frightened.* MAURA *tries to scream but* SCOTT *immediately puts his hand over her mouth to silence her and forces her to the sofa.* JAN *and* TOM *watch the scene play out,* JAN *horrified,* TOM *intrigued.)*

SCOTT. Shut up. Shut up. I'm warning you. Shut up!

*(*MAURA *stops struggling.)*

SCOTT. That's better. Now just hear what I have to say and then I'll go. I promise you. Okay?

(**MAURA** *nods her head.* **SCOTT** *releases her and tries to compose himself. He walks behind the sofa.*)

SCOTT. *(Cont.)* I sent a man to the gas chamber because of you.

MAURA. You sent a man to the gas chamber because he was guilty.

SCOTT. No. No he wasn't. In my heart I know he wasn't. There were still possibilities to prove him innocent. It could have been anyone. She could have been sleeping with other guys. It could have been a drug deal gone bad. There were possibilities, don't you understand? But you and the rest of those narrow-minded jurors didn't want to see that. And I gave up. I let it all go. Because the bottom line was I wanted to have you more than I wanted to save him. That's the power you have over me, Maura.

MAURA. Then that's your problem isn't it?

SCOTT. How heartless are you?

MAURA. I suspect you're finding out now.

SCOTT. *(Notices her bags.)* You're packing. Where are you going?

MAURA. I don't think it's any of your business.

(**SCOTT** *goes to her purse on the desk, pulls out the folded itinerary and begins to read it.* **MAURA** *tries to take it from him.*)

MAURA. *(Cont.)* Give me that.

(**SCOTT** *forcefully shoves her back as he looks it over.*)

SCOTT. Paris?

MAURA. Why not? I told you I was thinking about going there some day. Now seems just as good a time.

SCOTT. There's no return date. You weren't corning back. *(More menacing. He closes in on her.)* You conned me. You conned me, you bitch. You got exactly what you wanted from me and now you're walking out. *(He crumples the itinerary and throws it at her.)* Well, I won't be made a fool of. Not again. Not by you or anyone else. *(He begins pushing her back with short, powerful jabs.)* You're not walking out on me, Maura, you understand? I won't let you.

MAURA. Please, Scott, don't.

SCOTT. You let me into your life because I meant something to you. And now suddenly I don't. Do you think that's fair? You're not going anywhere. How could you think I would let someone I love so much get away from me? How could you even think that? *(He continues pushing her back towards the sofa)* How! How! How!

(He violently pushes her back down on the sofa. With his hands on her shoulders, he leans over her. The lights dim on them. Surreal lights up on **JAN** *and* **TOM**.*)*

JAN. He's over the edge. He's going to kill her this time, isn't he?

TOM. It's a possibility. It's always a possibility with these kind of people. They're so volatile, so erratic. You have no idea how many times I told Maura that. Sometimes you women just don't listen.

JAN. *(Rushing towards the door.)* I want to leave here. I really want to leave here.

TOM. *(Grabs* **JAN** *by the arm and sits her on the swivel desk chair, turning it so she faces the audience.)* You're just upset. Maybe a little wine might calm you. *(Offering the poisoned wine.)* Here. Have a sip.

JAN. No.

TOM. *(More forceful.)* I said have a sip. *(Even more forceful.)* Drink it! Drink it now!

(Frightened, **JAN** *takes a sip and puts the glass down on the desk.)*

TOM. *(Continuing.)* There. Isn't that better? Now finish reading.

*(*JAN *returns to reading the manuscript. The lighting on* **MAURA** *and* **SCOTT** *returns to normal.)*

SCOTT. I had hoped it would be different between you and me, Maura. I tried to reason with you. But it seems this is the only kind of reasoning you can understand.

MAURA. *(She pushes* SCOTT *away with her feet and tries to get to the door.)* Keep away from me, Scott.

*(*SCOTT *grabs her and swings her around.)*

SCOTT. I don't want to hurt you, Maura.

(He hits her in the face. She falls to the ground, sobbing.)

But this is to remind you that I can any time I want, do you understand?

*(*SCOTT *lifts her by her shoulders and throws her onto the sofa.)*

Do you?

MAURA. *(Weakly. Trying to control her crying.)* Yes. I understand.

SCOTT. Okay, let's talk about this like reasonable adults who for now are having, let's say, domestic difficulties. Now if we both try to be fair, try to show a little consideration for one another, a little kindness, it can all be reasonably worked out. It can all be put back together to where it was. I can be what I was at the beginning. Charming, caring. And you can be the same little shy, innocent girl I first met. We can have it all again, Maura. We really can.

MAURA. Otherwise?

SCOTT. *(Almost helpless.)* There can't be an otherwise, Maura. You know that.

MAURA. Yes, I know that. *(A beat. She has herself under control now. She rises from the sofa and goes to him.)* You're sorry when you hit me, aren't you, Scott?

SCOTT. *(In emotional pain.)* Yes, yes I am. But sometimes there's no other way.

MAURA. Yes. Yes, I know, dear Scott, I know.

SCOTT. Dear Scott. I like that.

MAURA. I know.

(Now trying to soothe him, she hugs him and tenderly strokes his head. During the following **TOM** *pours another glass of wine.)*

SCOTT. I always knew you were different than the others. They never loved me. But you do love me. That's why you won't leave me. Because you truly love me. And you forgive me.

MAURA. Yes, of course I do, Scott. Of course I forgive you.

SCOTT. *(Sweet. Apologetic.)* I swear, Maura. We'll have a good life together. I'll be so thoughtful and caring. I was actually doing really good until... until I thought you didn't love me anymore. And then you gave me no choice.

MAURA. *(Still soothing him.)* I know. *(A beat.)* I need a glass of wine. How about you?

SCOTT. Yes. I'd like one.

*(***SCOTT*** is emotionally drained.* **MAURA** *leads him to the sofa where he sits. She kisses him and then goes to* **TOM,** *who hands her the glass of wine he has poured.* **MAURA** *then takes the glass of poisoned wine from the desk, returns to* **SCOTT** *and hands him the poisoned wine. She then sits next to him and lifts her glass.)*

MAURA. To us.

SCOTT. Yes. Yes. To us.

(They clink their glasses and drink. **MAURA** *becomes quite strong.)*

MAURA. We're very gifted people Scott. You are gifted at finding vulnerable, needy women which you thought I was, and I seem to be gifted at getting involved with abusive men, which coincidentally but not surprisingly, you turned out to be. But you know what I seem to be more gifted at? Getting rid of them.

(She rises. **SCOTT** *sits motionless.)*

SCOTT. What are you talking about?

MAURA. *(During the following she gets a bag of M &M's from the kitchen and begins eating them.)* Believe me, Scott, I don't go out of my way to do what I do. In fact at the very beginning I had hopes this romance would work out. I truly did. And then when it didn't, well, I tried to warn you Scott. But you seem to be just as stubborn as the rest of them. And so I have to deal with you the only way I know how. The way I've been doing it in all the other places that didn't seem to work out for me. Chicago, Denver, San Francisco. My goodness, men like you seem to be everywhere, don't they? Try getting up, Scott.

SCOTT. I...I can't. I can't move.

MAURA. I tried to warn you, Scott. I tried to get you to back off. I really did.

SCOTT. My body. I can't...I can't feel it.

MAURA. Poor Scott. Poor, poor Scott.

(Surreal lighting on JAN *and* TOM. *Normal lighting on* MAURA *and* SCOTT *dims.)*

JAN. It's murder. Right or wrong, it's still murder.

TOM. I didn't see you trying to stop it. Maybe you wanted him dead too. A man never really knows what's in a woman's head.

JAN. But in this case, you do. In this case it's in your head.

TOM. Yes. Maybe.

(Normal lights up on SCOTT *and* MAURA. MAURA *takes the glass from* SCOTT's *hand and puts it on the coffee table.)*

MAURA. This poison that I use, Scott, has quite unique properties. First it paralyzes, then it kills. Which is quite preferable for my purposes because I want you bastards to know exactly who, what and why, which now you do. *(Sits next to him and begins stroking his head affectionately.)* Unfortunately, it does show up in the system and they will come looking for me. But they never will find me because it's quite easy to get lost in this world if you want to. In a few days I will have a different name, a different look and I will be somewhere else far, far away for a long, long time. This time Paris. Maybe there I'll finally meet someone nice, someone honest and mentally healthy. I am so tired of you sick-o's. And you, Scott, will be right here in this wonderful apartment rotting away until someone can't take the stench anymore and discovers your decomposing body.

(Surreal lighting on **TOM** *and* **JAN** *comes up.* **MAURA** *rises and takes the manuscript from* **JAN** *and waves it at* **SCOTT**.*)*

MAURA. You thought you knew how the Stanway Case would end in my story. Well, as you now know it goes on past the verdict. It goes right on to this moment, to this room. And guess what, Scott? You die in the end. You die, Stanway dies, and all's well that ends well. How do you like that? *(She drops the manuscript on the coffee table.)*

SCOTT. I think it stinks.

MAURA. *(She lifts* **SCOTT**'s *face in her hand.)* Oh, before I forget, Scott, darling, don't feel bad about Stanway. He was guilty. He really was. I told you. I saw him do it.

JAN. She gets away with it, doesn't she? Good for her. I'm glad. I'm really glad.

MAURA. *(Smiling, confident)* Yes, I do. I always get away with it, don't I Tom?

TOM. Yes, you do. But eventually everyone's luck runs out. I'm sorry, Jan. I didn't give you the last page.

MAURA. *(Alarmed. She confronts* **TOM**.*)* What last page? This is all there is to it. *(She holds up the manuscript to* **TOM**.*)* Scott dies, Stanway dies, and I go to Paris. For me, a very happy and satisfying conclusion.

TOM. Well, no, not really, Maura. Not this time. This time I felt like doing something different.

*(**TOM** takes the pad of paper that he was writing on from the desk and hands it to* **JAN**.*)*

TOM. *(Cont.)* Here. Read this.

> *(As* **JAN** *begins reading aloud from the pad,* **TOM** *faces* **MAURA** *who stands near the sofa.)*

JAN. For some reason, almost as if divine intervention had stepped in, Scott found the strength to lift his arms and grab Maura by the throat…

> **(TOM** *pushes* **MAURA** *down to the sofa so that* **SCOTT** *is able to wrap his arm around her neck. She lays face up on top of* **SCOTT** *screaming and kicking. She drops the manuscript to the floor.)*

MAURA. No! No! That's not how it happens. That's not how it ever happens!

JAN & TOM. And he squeezed and squeezed and squeezed.

SCOTT. I loved you so much.

> **(SCOTT** *strangles* **MAURA.** *Her body goes limp and then he too succumbs.)*

TOM. That's how they found them. She died in his death grip, unable to break away, unable to scream. Just able to die with him.

> *(The surreal lights brighten on* **JAN.** *She holds the pad towards* **TOM.** *)*

JAN. This is disgusting. This is the most vile thing I've ever read. *(She drops the pad on the desk in disgust.)* Just what the hell is the message… the point you're making?

TOM. That we live in a very warped society and no one really knows anyone anymore.

JAN. I need to go home. 1 need to get away from here.

TOM. Of course. You're finished with the story. I'm finished with you. You're free to go.

JAN. I…I can't.

TOM. What?

JAN. I can't move… My body, 1 don't feel it. The wine! Oh, no. I drank the wine!

TOM. *(Apologetic.)* Oh, oh, my God. I totally forgot. I'm so sorry. Forgive me. Wait, I'll fix it right up. *(He picks up the manuscript where* **MAURA** *dropped it, brings it to the desk, takes out a pencil and begins making adjustments in it.)* Here we go. We'll cross out the wine part and then at the end of my new page I'll just add… *(He switches to the pad and begins writing.* **JAN** *follows his instructions.)*

TOM. *(Cont.)* "His need for her being over, Jan rises…"

*(***JAN** *rises.)*

TOM. *(Cont.)* "…and thanks Tom for a wonderful evening…"

JAN. Thank you so much for a wonderful evening.

TOM. "Kisses him on the cheek…"

*(***JAN** *kisses* **TOM** *on the cheek)*

TOM. *(Cont.)* "…and leaves. Ta ta."

JAN. *(Goes to the door.)* Ta ta.

*(***JAN** *exits.* **TOM** *sighs, takes the pad of paper and pencil and stands behind the sofa. He looks at the dead bodies of* **MAURA** *and* **SCOTT**. *He thinks for a moment and then starts to jot something else down. During the following, the surreal lights begin to fade. A bright spot highlights* **TOM**'s *face.)*

TOM. As the bodies of Maura and Scott lay motionless on the sofa, the stage lights slowly fade. The end.

(He smiles. He is satisfied. The spot highlighting **TOM**'s *face fades out. The Stage is black.)*

THE END

COSTUME LIST

Prologue

Woman	Negligee
Man	All-black attire: pants, sweatshirt, shoes, and ski mask

Act I, Scene 1

Maura	Casual outfit suitable for jury duty, purse
Scott	Slacks, shirt and sport jacket
Jan	Casual outfit suitable for first date; skirt, blouse, purse
Tom	Slacks, shirt, sweater

Act I, Scene 2

Maura	Different casual outfit suitable for jury duty
Scott	Different, slacks, shirt and sport jacket
Jan	Same as Scene I
Tom	Same as Scene 1

Act I, Scene 3

Maura	Another jury duty outfit
Scott	Another jury duty outfit
Jan	A different casual outfit suitable for 2nd date, purse
Tom	Different slacks, shirt and sweater

Act II, Scene 1

Maura	Bathrobe over comfortable casual clothes, suitable for travel
Scott	Jeans, T-shirt, leather jacket. Jeans, a different T-shirt (no jacket)
Jan	Same clothes as previous scene
Tom	Same clothes as previous scene

PROP LIST

Prologue
    Hairbrush
    Styrofoam brick

Act I, Scene 1
    Keys on a key ring
    Automatic coffee maker
    Coffee
    Cream
    Sugar
    Spoons
    2 coffee cups
    Serving tray

Act I, Scene 2
    Keys on a key ring
    Bag containing take out food and a bottle of wine
    Corkscrew
    Silverware for two
    Napkins
    2 Plates
    2 Bottles of wine
    4 Wine glasses
    Letter-size Manila file folder labeled "The Stanway Case"
    Hand-written notes on 8.5 x 11-inch paper in the file folder
    Manuscript (preset under file folder)

Act I, Scene 3
    Keys on key ring
    Spare key (Scott)
    Bottle of wine
    Corkscrew
    Bag of groceries (Tom & Jan)

Act II, Scene I
    Container of yogurt
    Spoon
    8.5 x 11-inch note pad
    Spare key
    2 suitcases
    Purse with airline itinerary sticking out of pocket
    Bottle of wine
    2 wine glasses
    Small vial with liquid
    Corkscrew
    Small bags of M&M's
    Loose sheet of 8.5 x 11-inch paper in drawer

SET PIECES

2 Large Bookcases filled with books

Wine Rack on a shelf of a bookcase, filled with several
 bottles of wine

Sofa Bed

Coffee Table

2 Comfortable Side Chairs

Desk

Swivel Desk Chair

Desk Lamp

Computer

Printer

Telephone

Answering Machine

Pencil holder on desk, filled with pencils and pens

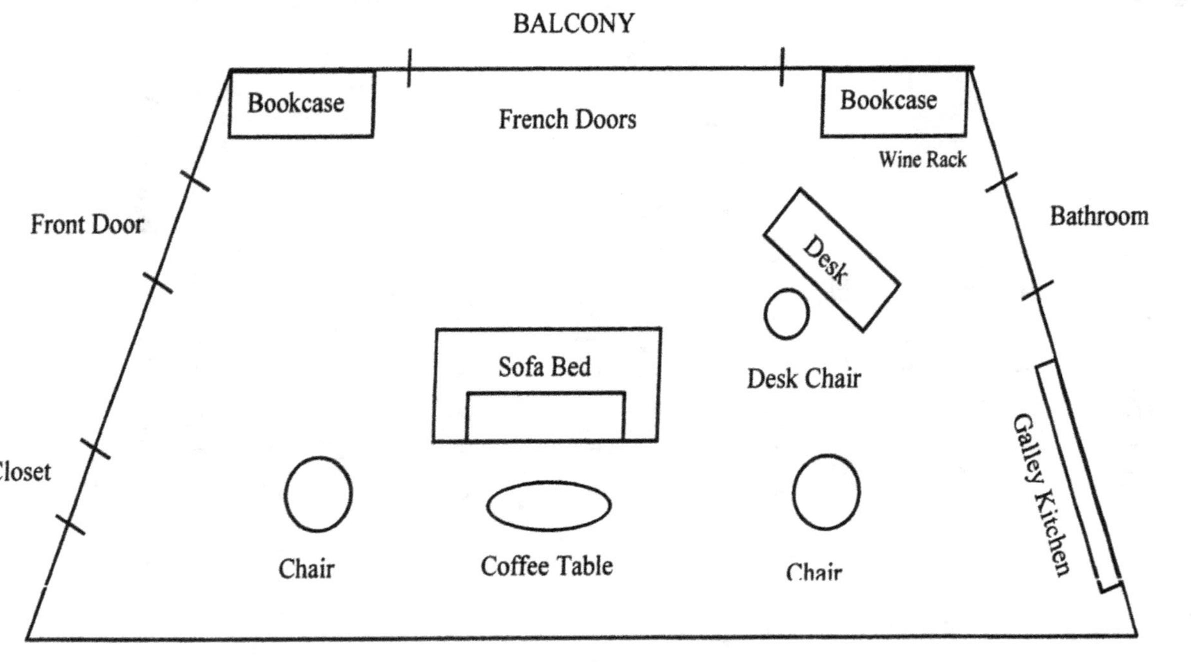

THE SPIDER OR THE FLY?
Set Design

Also by
Sam Bobrick...

Annoyance

Are You Sure?

Baggage

The Crazy Time

Death in England

Flemming (An American Thriller)

Getting Sara Married

Hamlet II

Last Chance Romance

New York Water

Passengers

The Psychic

Remember Me?

**Splitting Issues
(And Other Noteworthy Concerns)**

Please visit our website **samuelfrench.com** for complete
descriptions and licensing information.

OTHER TITLES AVAILABLE FROM SAMUEL FRENCH

THE PSYCHIC

Sam Bobrick

Murder Mystery, Comedy / 4m, 2f / Interior

Winner! 2011 Mystery Writers of America Edgar Allen Poe Awards – Best Play!

Adam Webster, a down-on-his- luck writer, in desperation to make the rent, has put a sign in his apartment window, "Psychic Readings $25". The characters it draws in lead into a tangled murder mystery of sorts in this hilarious original comedy.

"The play's clever, Pirandello-esque twists make for a pleasant divertissement…satisfyingly unpredictable"
– *Los Angeles Times*

"Surprise plot twists, and all-around hilarity. It's one of the best original comedies I've seen!"
–*StageSceneLA*

"A delightful murder mystery adventure…many humorous, suspenseful, unexpected twists and turns…Bobrick shows his innate ability with this play's sharp wit and impeccable comedic timing… audiences…will savor the suspense and surprise that
The Psychic delivers."
– *Tolucan Times*

"*The Psychic* is a laugh-filled unexpectedly entertaining ride that gratifies copiously from moment to moment."
– *Broadway World*

"Engaging, surprising, clever and funny!"
– *Examiner*

OTHER TITLES AVAILABLE FROM SAMUEL FRENCH

ARE YOU SURE?

Sam Bobrick

Comedy / 3m, 3f / Interior

Are You Sure? is a play of shifting realities. How much is happening? How much isn't? Does David want to kill Caroline? Does Charley want to kill David? Does Caroline want to kill everyone? The play mixes comedy with high suspense as the audience tries to figure out what and who to believe. One fact is certain: someone did do it.

"Sam Bobrick has used his considerable experience and dexterity as a playwright to thread the lines between the indefinite categories of reality and fantasy, gamesmanship and seriousness, even between theater and fact."
– Los Angeles Times

"A clever and literate theatrical Rubic's cube…Pick of the Week."
– L.A. Weekly

"A Chinese ring trick…Fantastical phantasmagoria."
– Dramalogue

"Lucidly crafted."
– Hollywood Reporter

OTHER TITLES AVAILABLE FROM SAMUEL FRENCH

DEATH IN ENGLAND

Sam Bobrick

Comedy / 5m, 3f / Single Set

Death pays a call to an English household and discovers he's in the wrong place. After apologizing profusely to the near victim, he discovers to his horror that not only can everyone in that household see him but that someone other than he is now performing his task. In an attempt to get to the bottom of things, none other than one of Scotland Yard's finest, Inspector Edward Mirabelle, is brought in to confront the bizarre event, witness a few deaths and hopefully solve what the inspector now describes as his favorite case.

OTHER TITLES AVAILABLE FROM SAMUEL FRENCH

GETTING SARA MARRIED

Sam Bobrick

Comedy / 3m, 3f / Interior

Sara Hastings is an unmarried lawyer in her mid-thirties, much too busy to get involved in any romance. Her Aunt Martha has decided to take matters into her own hands and find her a husband. Unfortunately, Aunt Martha's method of doing it amounts to having the prospective groom bopped over the head and brought to Sara's apartment. Aunt Martha's choice is Brandon Cates, a young man who handles her finances. Although Brandon is already engaged to be married, this does not deter Aunt Martha. After being bopped on the head a few times, having a temporary loss of memory and experiencing several instances of mouth-to-mouth resuscitation and a confrontation with a very angry fiancé, Brandon slowly comes to realize that Sara is really the girl for him.

www.ingramcontent.com/pod-product-compliance
Lightning Source LLC
Chambersburg PA
CBHW070415120726
47909CB00005B/1667